Spider-Man 2: Everyday Hero

SPIDER-MAN 2™

Everyday Hero

Adaptation by Acton Figueroa

Illustrated by Ivan Vasquez and Jesus Redondo

Based on the Motion Picture

Screenplay by Alvin Sargent

Screen Story by Alfred Gough & Miles Millar and Michael Chabon

Based on the Marvel Comic Book by Stan Lee and Steve Ditko

📖 HarperFestival®
A Division of HarperCollins Publishers

Keeping a secret is not easy.

I know that better than anyone.

I am Peter Parker.

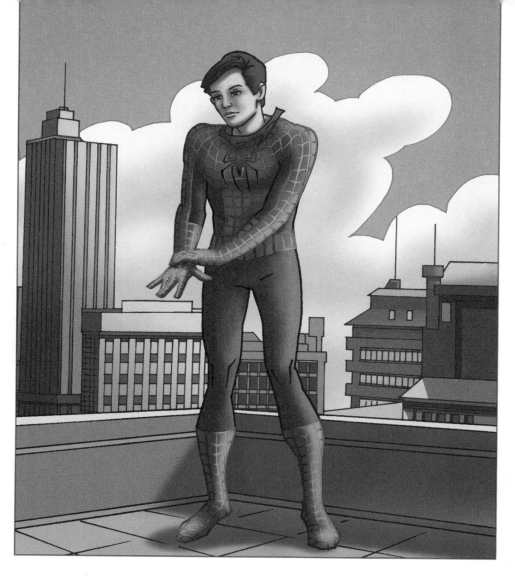

But when there is trouble,

I stop being Peter Parker.

I become Spider-Man.

That is my secret.

I am always watching out for danger.

And I find it almost every day.

I find out where the problem is.

I get there as fast as I can . . .

. . . and I take care of it.

Some robbers almost smashed

into this police car.

But I saved it in the nick of time.

I make sure that crime does not pay.

I do not stick around when my

job is done.

I am a busy guy.

I have a lot to do.

When I am Spider-Man, I can swing around the city on strands of webbing. As Peter Parker, I ride my motorbike.

But swinging on my webbing is
a lot faster than riding my motorbike.
So when there is trouble,
I put on my suit and get to work!

This truck is going much too fast.

But I can go even faster!

Next time, I hope
these kids remember
not to play in traffic.
They could get hurt.

Sorry, pal.

That camera does

not belong to you.

I love helping people, but keeping
my superpowers a secret is hard.

Keeping the secret from

Aunt May is especially hard.

Oh, no! It looks like there is some trouble at the bank.

Now that I have my Spider-Man
suit on, it is time to stop some more
bad guys.

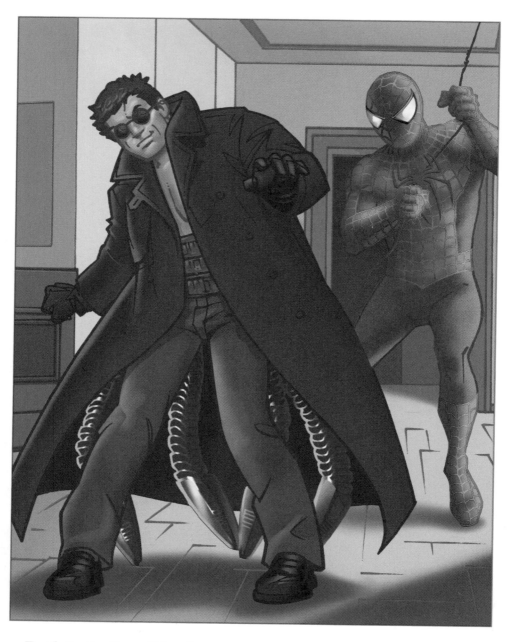

I think I will play a little joke on this
criminal and sneak up behind him.

It looks like the joke is on me!

Doc Ock!

Fighting a guy with so many arms is not
easy.

Now you are making me mad.

What kind of bully picks on a little kid?

Good catch!

Doc Ock had dropped her from a
window.

Every day, I am on the lookout for danger.

I keep nice people safe from harm.

I keep good people out of trouble.

Some people might call me a hero.

To me, I am just Peter Parker.

Unless someone is in danger,

and then I am Spider-Man.